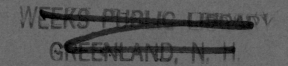

DARBY,
THE SPECIAL-ORDER PUP

DARBY

lively & affectionate

MOLLY

alert & willing

SOPHIE

saucy & sensitive

FEDORA

curious & eager

QUIGLEY'S AKC-REGISTERED ENGLISH BULL TERRIERS

Puppies available now to approved homes

*** OFFSPRING OF CHAMPIONS ***

Health guaranteed – Baer tested

INQUIRIES INVITED: Quigley Kennel, Kalamazoo, Michigan

Area Code: (616) 555-5555

SOLOMON

dependable & wise

McGUIRE

masterful & mannerly

BUCK

faithful & friendly

NACHO

clever & strong

DARBY
THE SPECIAL-ORDER PUP

Alexandra Day *&* Cooper Edens

pictures by Alexandra Day

Dial Books for Young Readers New York

Thanks to the Buck Family, Kyle Hendrix, Elisabeth Darling, Ted Gerontakos, Marilyn Bailey, Lynne Myall and Ch. Iceni Iambra's pups for their cheerful help. —A.D.

For Darby. —C.E.

Published by Dial Books for Young Readers
A division of Penguin Putnam Inc.
345 Hudson Street
New York, New York 10014

Designed by Nancy R. Leo-Kelly
The text for this book is set in Berkeley.
Printed in Hong Kong on acid-free paper
10 9 8 7 6 5 4 3 2 1

Library of Congress Cataloging in Publication Data
Day, Alexandra.
Darby, the special-order pup/by Alexandra Day and Cooper Edens;
pictures by Alexandra Day.
p.   cm.
Summary: The Bells have trouble training Darby, the puppy they
have ordered through the mail, but in the end he saves them from disaster.
ISBN 0-8037-2496-9 (hc.)
[1. Dogs—Fiction.] I. Edens, Cooper. II. Title.
PZ7.D32915Dar 2000 [E]—dc21 99-42632 CIP

The art was created using watercolor paints on watercolor paper.

"Dad, Mom, look . . . the place we went to last summer has puppies for sale. Could we get one, please . . . please?"

"Here he is, folks."

"This is your new home, Darby.
We hope you'll like it."

That night . . .

"Good night, Darby, boy. Sweet dreams."

The next afternoon . . .

"Mom! Dad! Come quick! You're not going to believe what Darby's done!"

"So, Mr. Quigley, you say it isn't unusual for one of your puppies to . . . you think it's just his way of exploring his new home, do you? . . . How soon will he grow out of it? . . . Two or three years! Yes, we can give him lots of extra love and attention. . . . Right . . . yes . . . I understand. . . . Thank you, Mr. Quigley."

"Darby, no!"

"We called Mr. Quigley again, and he says Darby just needs training. It says here that the owners are the best ones to train a dog. That way he learns to 'behave in the home environment.'"

"Darby, sit!"

Two weeks later . . .

"Darby, catch!

"Darby, speak!"

WOOF!

"Darby, fetch!"

"You kids have done a great job with Darby. He sure seems to be a changed dog."

"We're going to the movies, Darby. Behave yourself while we're gone."

WEATHER ALERT
In coastal areas,
heavy rains continue
to cause concern to
beachfront residents

"Now maybe we'll get some peace."

"How do you like it, Darby?"

A few days later . . .

"There, Darby, that's enough
  biscuits. Now go in your
  house—it's raining pretty hard."

"This is Linda Sorada, live at the scene of the embankment slide off Route 101. The Bell home has certainly been buried by the collapsing bank. Neighbors believe that the Bells were all home at the time of the disaster, and rescue workers are digging frantically from the beach to reach the trapped family."

"Don't worry, kids. Nobody's hurt, and we've got plenty of air."

"I'm sure there are rescuers coming to get us out."

"I'm hungry, Mom."

"Is the bathroom still working?"

"I doubt it."

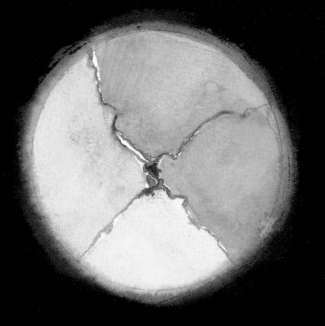

"Listen! There's something
going on behind the wall.
It's starting to crack!"

"Look! There's a hole now—
with something coming
through!"

"It's Darby! He found us!"

"Come on, kids, we can use Darby's tunnel to get out of here."

"Let's go, Darby. Show us the way!"

"Good boy, Darby!"

"This is amazing! Darby, the Bell family's bull terrier, has beaten the rescue workers to the job! This incredible dog tunneled his way down to his trapped family, and they are all safe on the surface!"